My Secret Love
by Andy Brown

by Narinder Dhami

Illustrated by Julie Anderson

CHAPTER 1

I'm In Love!!!!!!

I've been in love now since 8.43 a.m. on January 14th, and it feels GREAT.

Want to know how it happened?

I was walking to school that morning, like I always do. And I was feeling lousy, like I always do on a Tuesday. Well, I always feel lousy on Mondays, Wednesdays, Thursdays and Fridays too, but Tuesdays are just THE PITS. My first lesson is French with Mr Walkman. Walkman's a twit. My next lesson is Maths with Mrs Sims. She's an old dragon. Then I've got history with Mr Clarke. He's about 200 years old. So you can see why I was feeling lousy.

But I didn't know then that this was the day I was going to fall crazily in love. Not until I went round the corner into Church Street.

And there she was.

The Girl.

She was walking up the street towards me. I couldn't take my eyes off her. She was small and slim, and she had black hair and big, brown eyes. She was beautiful. She even looked good in her school uniform.

My heart went into overdrive, and started thumping like mad. My knees turned to mush. My mouth went dry.

Every second she was coming closer and closer and closer towards me ... As we passed each other, she looked at me, and I looked at her, and that was IT. I was in love.

When I got to the corner, I turned round for one last look. My heart began to race. The girl had turned round too, and was staring at me. Our eyes met again, and then she was gone.

I walked the rest of the way to school in a daze. Who was she? What was her name? I had to know. I knew she went to Brookside Girls' School because of her uniform. But that was all.

"Hi there, Andy," said a voice in my ear.

Why have you got that stupid wet look on your face?

I looked round. It was my best mate, Jaz.

"Oh, hi," I said, trying to look cool instead of stupid and wet.

Jaz stared at me.

"You look like you've just won a million quid," he said. "Come on, what's going on?"

I felt my face go red.

"Nothing," I said quickly. I didn't want to tell Jaz about The Girl. Not yet. "Have you got that CD I lent you?"

Jaz wasn't listening to me. He had more important things on his mind. Like the pretty girl with long, dark hair who was walking past us right at that very moment.

"Hang on a sec," he said. "I've just got to go and talk to that girl over there."

"Who is she?" I asked. "Do you know her?"

Jaz winked at me. "No, but I'd like to!"

Typical, I thought gloomily, as Jaz walked over to the girl and started talking to her.

That's Jaz all over. He can chat girls up standing on his head. Me, I can't even say hello to someone I like without making a fool of myself.

But I had a feeling that this time, things might be different.

I just hoped I would see The Girl again the next day ...

CHAPTER 2

I Saw The Girl Again!!!

I was really nervous the next morning. I felt so nervous I couldn't eat any breakfast.

"What's the matter with you?" asked my mum. "Are you feeling ill?"

"No, I'm fine," I said quickly. "I just don't want any breakfast, that's all."

"What?" said my mum. "But you always have two bowls of cornflakes, four pieces of toast and three cups of coffee before you go to school."

"I'm just not hungry, thanks," I said firmly.

My mum looked at me oddly.

"You're ALWAYS hungry. What's going on?"

I didn't answer. I just put on my jacket
and left in a hurry. Well, you can't talk to
mums about *love*, can you? They wouldn't
understand.

I got to Church Street at the same time as I
did the day before. I went round the corner.
And the girl was coming straight towards me.

I walked slowly down the street. I wanted
to stare at her, but I knew my face was as red
as a tomato. So I didn't dare look up. Instead I
stared down at my feet the
whole time. But I did
see one thing. She
had a school bag
over her arm, and
her name was written
on it. It was Beth.

Beth, I said to myself.
What a brilliant name.

Beth. It sounded like music in my head.
Beth. Beth. Beth. Beth. Beth. Beth.

I walked on down the road. At the corner, I stopped to look back. Beth had stopped too. And she was looking back at me... My heart started to thump like mad. Maybe she really did like me.

"You've got it again," said Jaz when I got to school.

"Got what?" I asked.

"That stupid wet look on your face." Jaz stared hard at me. "Is it a girl?"

"No," I said, trying to be cool. But he'd sussed me out all right.

"Come on, Andy!" he said, grinning. "I want to hear all about it. Who is she?"

"I don't know," I said. And I told him how I'd met Beth. Or rather, how I hadn't met her yet.

"I'll tell you what to do, Andy my man," Jaz said. "When you see her again, you've got to walk right up to her and say something."

You mean *talk* to her?

That's the best way to get to know someone.

"What will I say?" I wasn't sure I had the guts to go and talk to Beth. I felt so nervous every time I saw her.

"Ask her what the time is. That always works. Then you can start chatting her up. *Then* you can ask her out. Go on, mate. Go for it!"

Jaz was right. I just had to go for it.

The very next day.

I needed all the luck I could get.

CHAPTER 3

The Day I Went For It

I did a really, really stupid thing.

It was so stupid, I could die of shame. I suppose you lot are dying to know what happened.

I was all set to talk to Beth. I got to Church Street at the right time in the morning. And there she was, walking up the street. She had some books under her arm, and she looked gorgeous.

I walked towards her. My heart was beating like crazy. I was shaking all over. We were getting closer and closer and closer ...

I knew what I was going to say. "Excuse me, have you got the time, please?" I'd said it over and over again to myself in my head.

Now we were really close. Just a few metres apart. My heart was beating fit to bust. I opened my mouth –

And then it happened.

Suddenly Beth dropped one of her books. It was a big maths textbook. It fell on the pavement, right in front of me.

I tripped over it.

Can you believe that? What an idiot.

I went flying. I hit the ground with a crash, and banged my chin. I was so ashamed, I wished a big hole would open right there in front of me and swallow me up.

And you know what? Beth didn't even say "Are you OK?" She didn't say anything. She just picked up her book, and rushed off down the road.

Slowly I got to my feet. I wished I was dead.

Jaz was waiting for me when I limped into school.

"Well, I can see what happened," he said. "You asked Beth for a date, and she punched you on the chin."

"Oh, shut up," I snapped. "I've really gone and done it now." And I told him what had happened.

"Beth didn't even ask me if I was OK," I said gloomily. "She just doesn't like me."

Jaz started laughing. I felt like punching HIM on the chin.

"What's so funny?" I asked crossly.

"Come off it, Andy, you dipstick! Don't you know anything about women? Beth dropped that book on purpose!"

I stared at him.

"What?"

"Beth dropped that book on purpose," Jaz said again. "She was hoping you'd pick it up for her, and get talking."

"Really?" My mouth fell open. "You mean she likes me?"

Jaz nodded.

"I bet Beth feels really bad that you fell over," he said. "I bet she feels just as daft as you do right now."

A big smile lit up my face. I was feeling better already.

Beth liked me. She really did.

When I saw her again the next morning, I was going to ask her out.

And this time nothing was going to stop me ...

CHAPTER 4

The Great Day – Or Was It?

Friday was the Great Day. The day I was going to ask Beth for a date.

I got up early, and had a shower. I washed my hair. I ironed my school uniform. I even nicked some of my dad's aftershave.

As I put my books in my school bag, I practised over and over again what I was going to say to Beth.

"Hi. Have you got the time, please?"

"Hi there. Have you got the time, please?"

"Hi. Have you –?"

"You're talking to yourself again." My mum came into the kitchen. "What's the matter with you?"

"Nothing," I said quickly. Is your mum a right Nosy Parker too, or is it just mine?

"Well, sit down and have some breakfast before you go." My mum went over to the cooker. "Scrambled eggs OK?"

I felt sick.

"No thanks, Mum. I'm not hungry."

"Not hungry again?" she said. "This is serious."

"It's no big deal," I snapped. I didn't want to tell her about Beth. Not yet.

"I suppose it's some girl," said my mum. "Who is she?"

"Bye." I grabbed my bag, and ran out of the back door. Parents. They can beat Sherlock Holmes any day.

I ran all the way to Church Street. When I got to the corner, I stopped, took out a comb, and combed my hair. I had to look good for my big day.

I took a deep breath. I walked round the corner – and that was when I saw Beth.

With another boy.

She was walking up the road with him. They looked as if they knew each other well, because they were chatting and laughing. For a moment or two I stood at the corner. I was too shocked to move. Then I made myself walk forward, even though my legs felt like jelly.

The boy was tall, dark haired and quite good looking. I hated him. I wanted to stick my foot out and trip him up. Or maybe punch him on the nose. Hard.

I felt sick. Beth already had a boyfriend. I was too late.

We walked past each other. I didn't look at Beth. I don't know if she looked at me. I don't think so. She was having a much better time with Mr Tall, Dark and Handsome.

So that was that ...

"You look like you're about to kill somebody." Jaz met me in the playground. "What happened?"

"So you know all about women, do you?" I snapped at him. "Beth's already GOT a boyfriend."

"Yeah?" Jaz looked surprised. "How do you know?"

"She was walking with him this morning," I said miserably.

"And?" Jaz looked at me.

"And what?" I said.

"I mean, were they kissing?" asked Jaz. "Holding hands? Being all lovey-dovey?"

"No," I had to admit. "But he has to be her boyfriend. Who else could he be?"

Jaz looked at me.

"Her brother. Her cousin. A mate. The boy next door. He could be *anybody*."

"No." I shook my head gloomily. "He's her boyfriend. I know he is. Just my luck."

Jaz and I had got tickets for a concert by a local band called the Bald Eagles. I'd been looking forward to it for weeks. Now I didn't care if I went or not.

My life was over ...

CHAPTER 5

The Bald Eagles Gig

It was Saturday night. I was standing outside the hall where the Bald Eagles were playing, waiting for Jaz. He's never on time for anything. He'd be late for his own funeral.

There were loads of people around. The Bald Eagles are one of the best bands in our town, and everyone wanted to see them. There was a sign on the doors that said "Bald Eagles – sold out".

I walked up and down the street, kicking a Coke can around.

Guess what I was thinking about? You've got it. Beth.

I was still sure that she already had a boyfriend. But that didn't stop me from liking her. And I thought she liked me. Maybe I was wrong ...

I wasn't sure what to do now. I could walk to school a different way on Monday morning. But I didn't really want to do that.

I wish Beth was here right now, I thought miserably. I wish I knew if she likes me or not ...

I was just being stupid. But maybe I wasn't quite as stupid as I thought. Because when I looked up the street to see if Jaz was coming, I saw Beth.

My heart started to race. I could hardly believe my eyes. Beth was walking down the street towards me. She looked beautiful in jeans and a white shirt. And she wasn't with that other boy. She was with a gang of girls.

My mouth went dry as they came closer. Then Beth saw me. For a moment we stared at each other. And then she smiled shyly at me.

I smiled back. I felt so happy, I could have turned cartwheels up the street. Beth wasn't with that other boy tonight. And she'd smiled at me. It looked like that guy WASN'T her boyfriend after all. I could still ask her out.

Beth and her friends went up the steps and into the hall. I wanted to go in too. I wanted to talk to Beth right away. But I couldn't get in because Jaz had the tickets. I had to wait.

By the time Jaz turned up, I was just about ready to burst with excitement. I ran up to him, and grabbed his arm.

"Come on, let's get inside!"

"Oi!" Jaz pulled away from me. "Mind my new jacket!"

"Never mind your stupid jacket!" I was hopping from one foot to the other. "Beth's inside!"

"Oh, I get it." Jaz grinned. "I thought you said she had a boyfriend?"

"Just come on, will you?" I begged him. This time nothing was going to go wrong.

We went up the steps. Two large bouncers were standing at the doors. Both of them looked as if they could rip a car to pieces with their bare hands.

"Tickets, please," said one of them.

Jaz put his hand into his trouser pocket. Then he looked through his jacket pockets. Then he turned out his trouser pockets again.

"What's up?" I asked him. I had a
terrible, sick feeling in my stomach. I knew
what he was going to say before he said it.

CHAPTER 6

Jaz Does It Again

I'm not a violent person. But I was ready to kill Jaz on the spot.

"What?" I yelled at him. "You can't have lost the tickets!"

"Well, I haven't got them." Jaz started going through all his pockets again. "I must have dropped them on the way."

I put my head in my hands. My luck was going from bad to worse. Beth was in there, and I was stuck out here.

"I don't believe this!"

"Look, don't panic." Jaz gave me a cool smile. "I'll get us into the gig. No problem."

"How?" I moaned. "It's sold out."

"You know me. I can talk my way into anything," Jaz said. "Watch this."

He went up to one of the bouncers (the one with the broken nose).

"Excuse me ..."

"Yeah?" said the bouncer grimly.

"My friend and I seem to have lost our tickets," said Jaz with a smile. "Could you let us in anyway?"

The bouncer folded his arms.

"What's it worth?"

Jaz put his hand in his pocket, and pulled out a paper bag.

ER – a bag of chocolate toffees?

The bouncers started laughing.

"On your bike, kid," said the other one (who had muscles twice as big as Arnie Schwarzenegger's). "No ticket, no entry."

"Great!" I said. "What do we do now?"

"Leave it to your Uncle Jaz, OK?" Jaz said calmly. "Just follow me."

He walked off round the side of the building. Gloomily I followed him.

"Where are we going?"

"Round to the back." Jaz stopped. He took a quick look round to make sure no one was watching. "We might be able to get in through a window."

We went round behind the hall. There were dustbins and cardboard boxes full of rubbish there. It smelt disgusting. But Jaz was right. One of the windows was open a little way.

Jaz pushed a dustbin over to the window, and climbed on to it. He looked inside.

"I think it opens into the loos," he said to me. "Come on. There's no one around."

I didn't like it much. But I had to get inside and see Beth. Anyway, we weren't doing anything wrong. Not really. After all, we HAD paid for our tickets ...

Jaz climbed through first. Then I followed. We were inside one of the loos. Jaz opened the door and peeped out.

"OK," he said. "Come on."

We tiptoed out, past the washbasins towards the door. Suddenly there was a loud scream. We both nearly jumped out of our skins.

We were in the loos all right. The GIRLS' loos. And there was a girl at the washbasins, washing her hands.

"Run for it!" Jaz said in my ear.

We legged it out of the girls' loos, and into the hall. There were loads of people in there, so I felt safe. The girl might go and tell the bouncers we came in through the window, but they'd never find us in the crowd.

"That was close," I said to Jaz.

"Told you I'd get you in," Jaz said. "Come on, let's find a good place to see the band."

"Not yet." I looked around. "You can help me to find Beth first."

There were so many people in the hall, it was hard to move. But we started looking. At last I spotted her. She was standing with her friends at the side of the hall.

"There she is!" I said to Jaz.

Jaz looked Beth up and down.

"Mmm, not bad," he said.

"Hands off!" I told him with a grin. "She's mine!"

"So, what are you waiting for?" Jaz slapped me on the back. "Get over there!"

"What about her mates?" I said. I didn't want them standing around and giggling at me.

"I'll talk to them." Jaz grinned at me. "You just chat up Beth. Come on."

"Yeah. OK." My heart was beating like crazy. This was it. The moment I'd been waiting for had come at last. I was going to ask Beth for a date ...

I walked over to her. Well, I tried to. But suddenly I couldn't move. A hand was holding my shoulder so hard, it hurt. Then I was spun round like a top. I was looking straight into the face of the bouncer with the broken nose. He had Jaz in one hand, and me in the other.

"That's them!" said the girl from the loos, who was with the bouncer. "They came in through the window!"

"Well, they're going out again through the door," growled the bouncer. And he frog-marched Jaz and me towards the exit.

Bye-bye, Beth ...

CHAPTER 7

Promises, Promises

By the next Monday morning, I'd made a promise.

I'd promised myself that if I didn't get a date with Beth that day, I'd give up. Simple as that.

"So do you want any breakfast this morning?" asked my mum. "Or are you still lovesick?"

"I am not lovesick," I said crossly.

My mum smiled.

"Do you want to ask Beth to tea on Sunday?"

"B-B-Beth?" I stammered. "I don't know any girls called Beth."

My mum started to laugh.

"Oh, really?" she said.

I looked down at the kitchen table. My history notebook was lying on it. And on the cover was a big red heart with "Andy Loves Beth" written inside it.

I turned bright red, and ran out of the door. Everyone seemed to know I fancied Beth. I had to get my act together. Fast.

OK, now I was ready. Ready for anything. When I saw Beth again, I was going to go right up to her and ask her out. Really and truly.

Well, I got to Church Street at the same time I always did. And you won't believe what happened.

Nothing.

That's right. Nothing. Nothing happened, because Beth wasn't there.

I checked my watch, just to be sure I was on time. I was. Then I went to the corner of the road, and looked up and down. She was nowhere to be seen. I waited for ten minutes, just in case she was late. But Beth didn't come.

I waited in Church Street for so long, I was nearly late for school. I got there just before the bell. Jaz was even later that I was. He ran through the gate just as the bell rang.

"Andy!"

I walked off. But he came after me.

"Did you see Beth today?" he asked me.

I shook my head.

"She wasn't there."

"Look," said Jaz. "I feel pretty bad about what happened at the gig."

"Good!" I snapped.

"So what if I meet you in Church Street tomorrow morning?" Jaz said. "I can fix you up with Beth. No problem."

"I can fix up my own date with Beth, thanks!" I muttered.

Jaz started to laugh.

"Come off it, Andy! You're too nervous. You need someone to do the talking for you. Someone like me."

I thought about it. Jaz was right. I wasn't doing very well on my own.

"Well, OK," I said at last. "But you'd better not mess things up for me this time!"

But Jaz didn't get a chance to fix me up with Beth. Because on Tuesday morning, Beth didn't turn up.

I didn't see her on Wednesday either.

Or Thursday ...

Or Friday ...

As I waited for Jaz in Church Street on Friday morning, I was miserable. Where had Beth got to? Was she walking a different way to school now? Maybe she didn't like me after all ... But, then, she'd smiled at me at the gig. Did she like me or didn't she?

Jaz came down the street towards me.

"Have you seen her today?"

I shook my head.

"Nope. Let's forget it."

Jaz was grinning at me like a mad thing.

"Hang on a sec. Wait till you see what I've got for you!"

Jaz put his hand in his pocket. Then he pulled a piece of paper out, as if he was a magician pulling a rabbit out of a hat.

"Look." Jaz pushed the paper into my hand. There was an address written on it.

62 Martins Way. What's this?

"It's Beth's address." Jaz looked smug. "I know a girl whose sister goes to Brookside Girls' School. She told me where Beth lives."

My face broke into a big smile. Suddenly that piece of paper was the best thing in the whole world.

"Thanks, Jaz!"

"OK, this is what you do," he said. "You go to Martins Way tomorrow. And you hang around outside Beth's house until she comes out. Then –"

"I chat her up!" I said eagerly.

"Right!" said Jaz. "I hope this works."

"It will!" I told him.

This is it, I thought. I just can't fail this time.

Can I?

CHAPTER 8

Waiting For Beth

On Saturday morning, I got up early. I was in the bathroom for about two hours, making myself look good. When I came out, Mum was outside the door.

"Seeing Beth today, are we?" she said with a grin.

I didn't answer. I went into my bedroom to get dressed.

It took me an hour to decide what to wear, but at last I was ready. I got on my mountain bike, and cycled to Martins Way.

Martins Way was a long, wide road. I cycled slowly along, looking for Number 62. There it was! I got so excited, I almost crashed into a lamp post.

I got off my bike and sat down on a wall.
I had a magazine with me, and I pretended to
read it. But really I was watching Beth's
house all the time.

"Can I have a go on your bike?"

I jumped. A ginger-haired kid was
standing next to me. He was about nine years
old, and he had a tatty BMX bike with him.

I gave him a dirty look.

"Are you kidding? Get lost. I'm trying to read my magazine."

The kid stuck his tongue out at me. Then he got on his bike and did a wheelie down the road.

"Your magazine's upside-down, birdbrain!" he yelled back at me.

I quickly turned my magazine the right way up. Then I glanced over at Beth's house again. When would she come out? And what was I going to say to her when she did?

I looked at my watch. It was twenty to ten.

It had started to rain. And now I was feeling cold. I zipped up my jacket, and looked at my watch again. It was eleven o'clock. No one had even come out of the house yet. How long would I have to wait?

It was getting colder. I shivered, and glanced at my watch. It was now ten past twelve. Where was she?

"Hey, why are you still here?" said a voice from behind me.

I looked round. The ginger-haired kid had come back with two of his mates. They were all staring at me.

"Look, just get lost, will you?" I said to them.

"He's been here for ages," said the kid to his friends.

"Maybe he's a burglar," said one of them.

"Yeah," said the ginger-haired kid. "I think we should call the police."

"I am not a burglar!" I snapped at them. "I'm just waiting for someone."

"Bet it's a girl!" said Ginger. And they all started giggling.

"Has she stood you up then?" said one of the others. And they laughed even more.

"Look, just beat it right now!" I yelled at them. They ran off, laughing. Then they got on their bikes, and cycled off down the road.

I looked at my watch again. It was one o'clock. It was pouring with rain by now. And I still hadn't seen Beth.

And then the door of Number 62 opened ...

I jumped up from the wall, my heart racing. At last! Beth was going to come outside.

But it wasn't Beth. A woman looked out, and put an empty milk bottle on the step. Then she went back in, and closed the door.

I looked at my watch again at half-past two. I was cold and wet through, and miserable.

"Look, there's the burglar! He's still here!"

It was the ginger-haired kid again. And this time he'd come back with about ten other kids. They were all looking at me, and giggling.

That did it. I'd had enough. I was cold and wet and I was fed up with horrible brats laughing at me. I had to face up to it. Beth and I were never going to get together, and that was that.

Sadly I got on my bike, and cycled home. From now on I was going to forget all about Beth.

And this time I meant it ...

CHAPTER 9

I'm Off Girls For Good!

On Monday morning, I felt terrible. My eyes hurt, my nose hurt, my whole body hurt. But I dragged myself out of bed and got ready for school.

Mum looked at me hard. "Have you got a maths test today or something?" she asked.

Mum never lets me stay home from school unless I'm dying.

"No," I said. I sneezed. "I think I'm getting a cold."

"Hmm," said my mum. "Well, if you're really ill, you'd better not go to school."

I sneezed again. And again.

"I want to go to school today, Mum," I said grimly. There's someone I've got to kill ..."

I walked to school, feeling lousy. I didn't see Beth. (Not that I was looking for her.)

"Blimey, you look terrible," Jaz said to me when I went into class. "Have you got a cold or something?"

"Yeah, I have," I said angrily. "Thanks to you. I stood in the cold and the rain for hours outside Beth's house. And I didn't even SEE her!

"Oh ..." Jaz looked embarrassed. "I have to tell you something, Andy."

"If it's one of your brilliant ideas – forget
it!" I snapped.

Er – Number 62,
Martins Way. That isn't
Beth's house ...

WHAT?!!

"Sorry. I was given the wrong address,"
Jaz said quickly.

"You mean – you mean I waited for five
hours outside the wrong house?" I said.

"Yeah. But don't worry." Jaz grinned at
me. "I can get you the right address."

"No!" I said weakly. "I don't want it."

"But –"

"JAZ, FORGET IT!" I shouted at him as loudly as I could. "I'm not going out with Beth. I'm not going out with ANYONE! I'm off girls for GOOD, understand?"

CHAPTER 10

Could This Be Love?

The next morning, I felt really ill. I didn't just have a cold. I had 'flu. Even Mum looked a bit worried. She put her hand on my head. Then she took my temperature.

"I think you'd better go to the doctor's," she said.

"Oh, Mum!" I groaned. Doctor Robinson is about 200 years old, and talks to me as if I was five. "I'll be fine."

"You're going to the doctor's, Andrew, and that's that," said my mum. "Do you want me to come with you?"

"Oh, Mum – PLEASE!" I sneezed again. "I'm old enough to go to the doctor's on my own."

I got out of bed. I ached all over, and my head hurt. I went over to the mirror, and looked at myself. My eyes were red, my nose was red, and my hair was sticking up. I looked a mess. It was a good thing Beth couldn't see me now.

But I wasn't going to think about Beth any more ...

I felt too ill to have a wash or clean my teeth. I just put on a pair of old jeans, and a

tatty sweatshirt. I didn't even comb my hair. I
was too ill to care what I looked like.

"The doctor can see you this morning."
Mum put down the phone. "But you'll have
to get there quickly."

I set off. But I felt so bad, I could only
walk slowly. A tortoise with a bad foot could
have got there quicker than I did.

The doctor's surgery was dark and
gloomy. It was the sort of place that made
you feel worse than you already did.

"Yes?" snapped the doctor's receptionist.

"Andrew Brown," I said weakly. "I'm here to see Doctor Robinson."

You're two minutes late, Sit down, and wait for your turn.

I looked round the waiting-room. Everybody in there looked awful. They were coughing or sneezing or groaning. And the room was packed. There wasn't a single empty seat left.

Except one. And it was next to a girl. A small, slim girl with long dark hair, and big brown eyes. She had a box of tissues on her knees, and she was blowing her nose.

IT WAS BETH!

I stared at her. She looked up and saw me, and her eyes lit up. She smiled.

I walked across the waiting-room towards her, and sat down. Even though I was wearing my old jeans and I hadn't combed my hair, I didn't care.

"Hi," we both said at the same time.

"How are you?"

Then we both sneezed. We looked at each other and burst out laughing.

"I've got this awful 'flu," she said. "I've been away from school for a week."

"I know," I said. "I mean, I didn't see you in Church Street like I usually do."

Beth smiled at me. I still felt ill, but I also felt wonderful. It was weird.

"My brother had the flu first, and I got it from him," she said. "He never gives me anything nice!"

"Your brother ..." I said. "Is he the boy you walk to school with sometimes?"

Beth nodded. I wanted to stand up and cheer. OK, now I could go for it, and ask her out. I know I've said this before. But this time NOTHING was going to stop me!

"Beth," I said, "will you –"

I sneezed.

"Will you –"

I sneezed again.

"Will you –"

I tried to say "Will you go out with me?"
But I just couldn't stop sneezing.

"Here, have a tissue," said Beth. "And
yes, I will go out with you!"

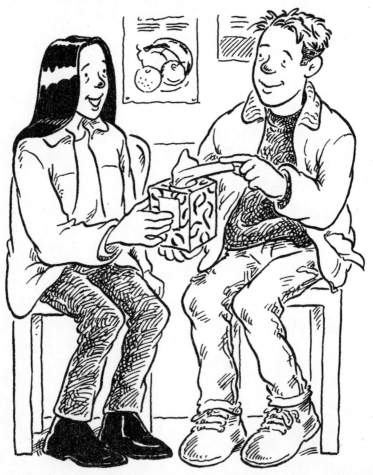